DEXTER BEXLEY
AND THE BIG BLUE BEASTIE ON THE ROAD

For Andrea

Some other books by Joel Stewart:

DEXTER BEXLEY AND THE BIG BLUE BEASTIE

ADDIS BERNER BEAR FORGETS

HAVE YOU EVER SEEN A SNEEP?
(written by Tasha Pym, illustrated by Joel Stewart)

For older readers, the Stanley Wells Mysteries:

THE TROUBLE WITH WENLOCKS

TREE SOUP

DEXTER BEXLEY AND THE BIG BLUE BEASTIE ON THE ROAD
A PICTURE CORGI BOOK 978 0 552 56112 9

First published in Great Britain by Doubleday,
an imprint of Random House Children's Books
A Random House Group Company

Doubleday edition published 2010
Picture Corgi edition published 2011

1 3 5 7 9 10 8 6 4 2

Copyright © Joel Stewart, 2010

Set in Joel 1 Regular

Picture Corgi Books are published by Random House Children's Books,
61–63 Uxbridge Road, London W5 5SA

www.kidsatrandomhouse.co.uk

Addresses for companies within The Random House Group Limited can be found at:
www.randomhouse.co.uk/offices.htm

THE RANDOM HOUSE GROUP Limited Reg. No. 954009

A CIP catalogue record for this book is available from the British Library.

Printed in Singapore

DEXTER BEXLEY

AND THE BIG BLUE BEASTIE ON THE ROAD

JOEL STEWART

PICTURE CORGI

Dexter Bexley and the Big Blue Beastie hooted

"AND THERE'S SO MUCH HOOTING TO DO,"

said the Big Blue Beastie.

So they hooted

and hooted,

until . . .

Dexter Bexley and the Big Blue Beastie
in the deep dark forest . . .

. . . hooted,

hooted

and hooted!

Dexter Bexley and the Big Blue Beastie hooted,

hooted . . .

. . . and hooted!

Until . . .

Dexter Bexley

and the Big Blue Beastie

and Princess Philippina

all hooted

together!

Until . . .

"IS IT TIME FOR OUR WEDDING YET?"

asked the tremendously charming Sir Percy Pecket.

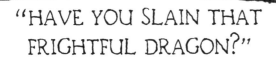

asked Princess Philippina.

"WE'RE NOT BUSY!"

said Dexter Bexley.

Dexter Bexley and the Big Blue Beastie and
Princess Philippina went to slay the Frightful Dragon.

But the Frightful Dragon wasn't really frightful
after all, so Dexter Bexley and the Big Blue Beastie and
Princess Philippina taught him how to tap dance.

The Frightful Dragon had talent.

Dexter Bexley and the Big Blue Beastie and Princess Philippina
and the Frightful Dragon became wandering players.

Dexter Bexley and the Big Blue Beastie and Princess Philippina
and the Frightful Dragon wandered

and played

and sang

and told tall tales

from one end of the kingdom to the other.

Then they wandered and played and sang
and told tall tales all the way back . . .

. . . until they stood at the Frightful Dragon's front door.

Luckily, the tremendously charming Sir Percy Pecket arrived and sang the song he'd sung for Princess Philippina on Tuesday.

It was a beautiful lullaby.

Dexter Bexley and the Big Blue Beastie and
Princess Philippina and the Frightful Dragon
stopped still to listen.

Then they yawned

and stretched

and . . .

. . . fell wonderfully, silently asleep.

Until . . .